BAXTER BUS
Epic Beach Day

by

Shaun Sturz

Foreword

When Shaun Sturz comes into contact with kids...smiles just happen. That's because he hasn't lost the "kid" inside of himself and kids relate to him instantly. It's a lot of fun to watch how he encourages kids to reach their full potential through the games they play and also just by the patience and respect that he shows each child that he comes in contact with. He encourages kids to develop respect, not only for themselves but for the other person as well. I don't think there is anything more important for a child than a good sense of self and Shaun really nurtures this quality in all the kids that are lucky enough to have the opportunity to hang out with him. And it all happens with lots and lots of smiles.

-Kenny G *Grammy Award Winning Artist*

Mom and Dad, thanks for always having Bu's back, woof!

Kurt, you are the coolest bro a bro can have.

Lyndie, thanks for being an inspiration and
sharing your life over the years with me.

Kenny, your support and kind words has hit a high note with me,
thanks man!

Max and Noah, the brothers I always wanted but never had. You rock!

Greg Griffith, you are the best art day companion a Bu could ask for!

Noah and Baxter Bu, Bu for short, are the world's best friends.

They do everything together.

Well, almost everything...

guard dog

Noah had become a beach bum, spending lots of time at the beach without Bu.

"Stay here Bu and guard the treehouse," Noah would say day after day.

2

As the summer days grew longer Bu decided he could not sit at home wagging his tail forever.

He was going to learn how to surf no matter how hard it was. He was determined to go surfing with Noah.

Bu quickly learned he was not the best swimmer— not even a fair swimmer. His legs were too short.

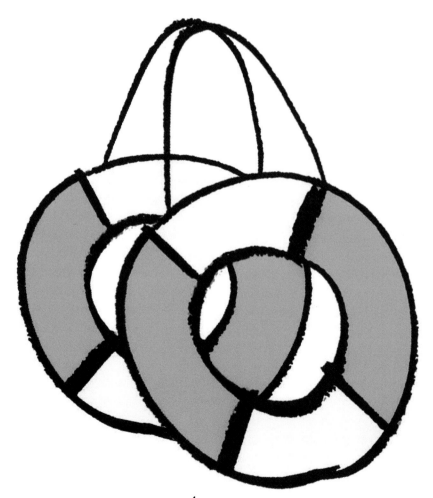

He shouted to a huge blue whale to see if he could teach him how to surf. The whale replied, "No, not today," and swam away.

He whispered to a
sleepy sea turtle,
"Please teach me how
to surf."

"Nooooo,"
snapped the sea turtle.

He then cornered a colony of crabs to see if they would teach him how to surf "No. No. No. No. No," as they scurried along.

His dreams of learning how to surf were quickly washed away, like the incoming tide.

An epic failure, that's what he was. A no-good, can't-surf, friendless dog. Who would want to be his friend anyway?

As Bu looked up, believing there was no luck at all coming his way, he saw something offshore.

He saw a surfboard headed directly at him moving super fast through the crashing waves.

KABOOM

"Sorry, Bro!" said a mysterious voice from behind the surfboard.

"I was telling you to get out of the way so you wouldn't get dinged in the head, but you didn't listen. My name is Bella Luck."

"Luck is your last name?" said Bu.

"Yes sir!" Bella replied. "I come from a very lucky family."

"This is not the type of luck I had in mind."
"I'm Baxter Bu, but my friends call me Bu."

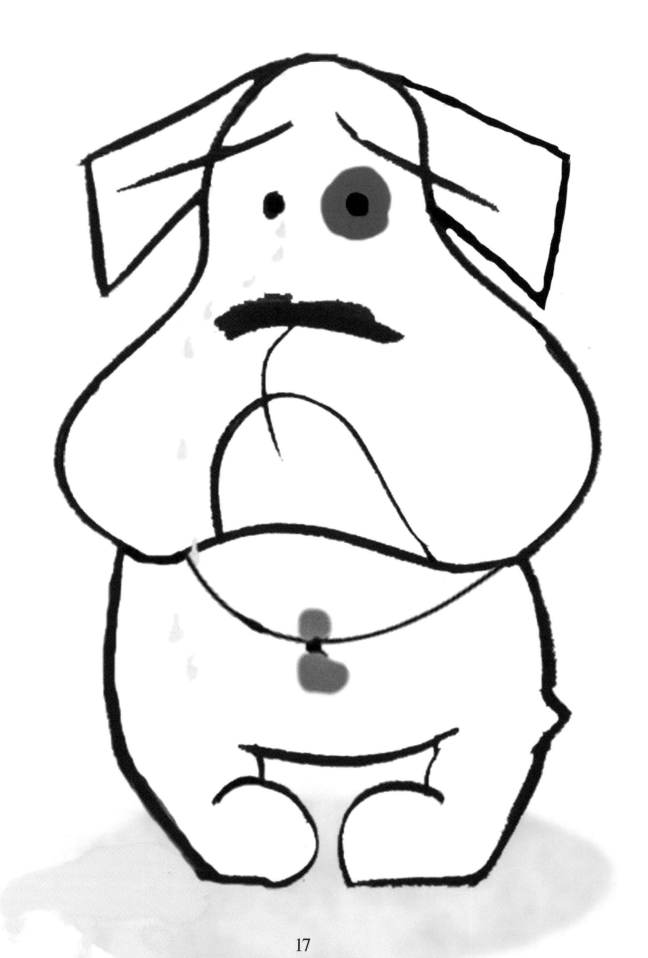

"Pleasure to meet you Baxter Bu, but may I suggest you keep on trotting. This is My surf spot, don't you see my paw prints everywhere on this beach? You groms are always on my beach."

"Don't worry you can have your spot. I'm not really a surfer and I botch everything up anyway."

Bella thought for a few seconds.

"Bu, you want to give it a go? I can teach you."

"YES! There is nothing I want more."
Bu quickly got amped up for his surf lesson.

This was turning out to be his lucky dog-gone day!

19

He wiggled his way onto the back of Bella's longboard as it was being steered into the oncoming swell. Bu realized this was all a balancing act, just like when he skateboarded with Noah.

Then he saw a HUGE wave rolling right toward him!

21

"Stop acting like a kook," Bella said while pulling Bu back up onto the longboard. "Dude, you really MUST focus. Just follow my lead. It's time to get psyched Bu. Get ready...

Banzai!"

The two of them caught a perfect party wave to shore, hanging ten the entire time. The waves were crashing and the wind was blowing so hard it went right through Bu's whistle and it sounded all the way into the shore. Noah heard this from the treehouse and came running to the shore as fast as he could.

"What happened Bu? I was worried when I didn't see you guarding the treehouse. Then I heard your whistle blow and I knew you were close. Why didn't you blow your whistle earlier? I would have found you sooner," said Noah trying to catch his breath. "That's why we have matching 'best friend' whistles, so we can always find each other."

Bu looked down at his whistle and realized his best friend had never really left him.

27

He was happy to have dog's best friend by his side yet again.

"You sure looked like the Big Kahuna out on that gnarly wave Bu!"

Bu looked at Bella and asked what "banzai" meant.

Bella smiled "It means total happiness."

Bu wagged his tail and barked,

The end

Definitions

Amped - excited, stoked

Beach bum - a person who spends hours and hours at the beach.

Botch - a person who screws things up.

Big Kahuna - the best surfer dude on the beach.

Banzai - a yell of excitement or joy; can also say Cowabunga.

Ding - a dent or nick, hit or strike.

Epic - near perfect, amazing

Gnarly - extreme, or dangerous

Grom - a younger inexperienced person.

Hang ten - to ride with the toes over the nose of the board.

Kook - somebody who does something weird or unusual; crazy, poser.

Longboard - a longer than usual surfboard; easier to surf on.

Party wave - a wave with lots of surfers on it.

Psyched - to be excited about something.

Wipe out - to fall off or be knocked off the surfboard.

About the Author

Born and raised in Bakersfield, CA, Shaun Sturz moved to Los Angeles after receiving his BA in Studio Arts from Westmont College. He is best known for his role on "Beverly Hills Nannies" on ABC Family. Shaun started his celebrity Manny career for saxophonist and Grammy winner, Kenny G's family. Shortly after, Shaun was asked by Brooke Burke of ABC's "Dancing With the Stars" to be a blogger for her popular mommy site, Modernmom.com. He gave advice and shared fun stories from his perspective as a male nanny. Los Angeles Magazine noted him as the top Manny in Beverly Hills. During these years as a Manny, Shaun realized that he could put his artistic talents to work and thus decided to write and illustrate his first children's book, "Baxter Bu's Epic Beach Day". This book is appropriately titled after Kenny G's lovable family dog.

www.ShaunSturz.com
@shaunsturz

Published by: Shaun L. Sturz

Cover and interior illustrations by: Shaun L. Sturz

Digitally designed by: Telemachus Press, LLC

ISBN 978-1-942899-23-5 (eBook)
ISBN 978-1-942899-24-2 (hardback)

2015.07.28

CPSIA information can be obtained at www.ICGtesting.com
Printed in the USA
LVIW01n1759300715
448166LV00004B/4